OO!

Illustrated by the artistic genius
Tony Ross

HarperCollins *Children's Books*

At the top
of the world lived
a very cheeky polar bear.

He was only little
but he **loved**
giving the other animals

a big
fright.

Slowly and silently he would creep up behind them
before going…

as the little cub would roll around

hooting with laughter.

The little cub's mama
would ask him
time and time again,

"How would you
like it if someone went
boo to you?"

But he wouldn't listen.

All the little cub
longed for was to be
big and **fearsome**
like his papa.

One morning a helicopter was spotted in the sky.
News spread across the ice that a man
was coming to the Arctic to make a

TELEVISION SHOW.

The animals were going to be

FAMOUS

They began making themselves
look beautiful for the cameras.

A wrinkly walrus wanted to top up his tan. He decided to sunbathe in the nude.

The little cub crept up…

behind the walrus…

The walrus was so shocked he *kicked up* his back flippers.

His tusks became skis as he *zoomed* across the snow.

WWWHHHIIIZZZZ...!

Meanwhile a platoon of puffins preened their feathers.
Time to do Boo Two.

"BOO!"

"Caw!"

"Caw!"

"Caw!"

Startled, the puffins all
tried to take flight at once.

Wings **walloped**.

Beaks **bashed**...

"Caw!"

"Caw!"

"Caw!"

"Caw!"

and the poor birds crashed headfirst into an iceberg.

WALLOP!!!

There was no stopping the little cub now.

Next he sawed a hole in the ice sheet with his paw, before diving down into the freezing water below.

Time to do an **underwater boo**.
But to who?

The little cub spied a pair of killer whales practising a *synchronised swimming routine,* ready for the cameras.

"Boo!"

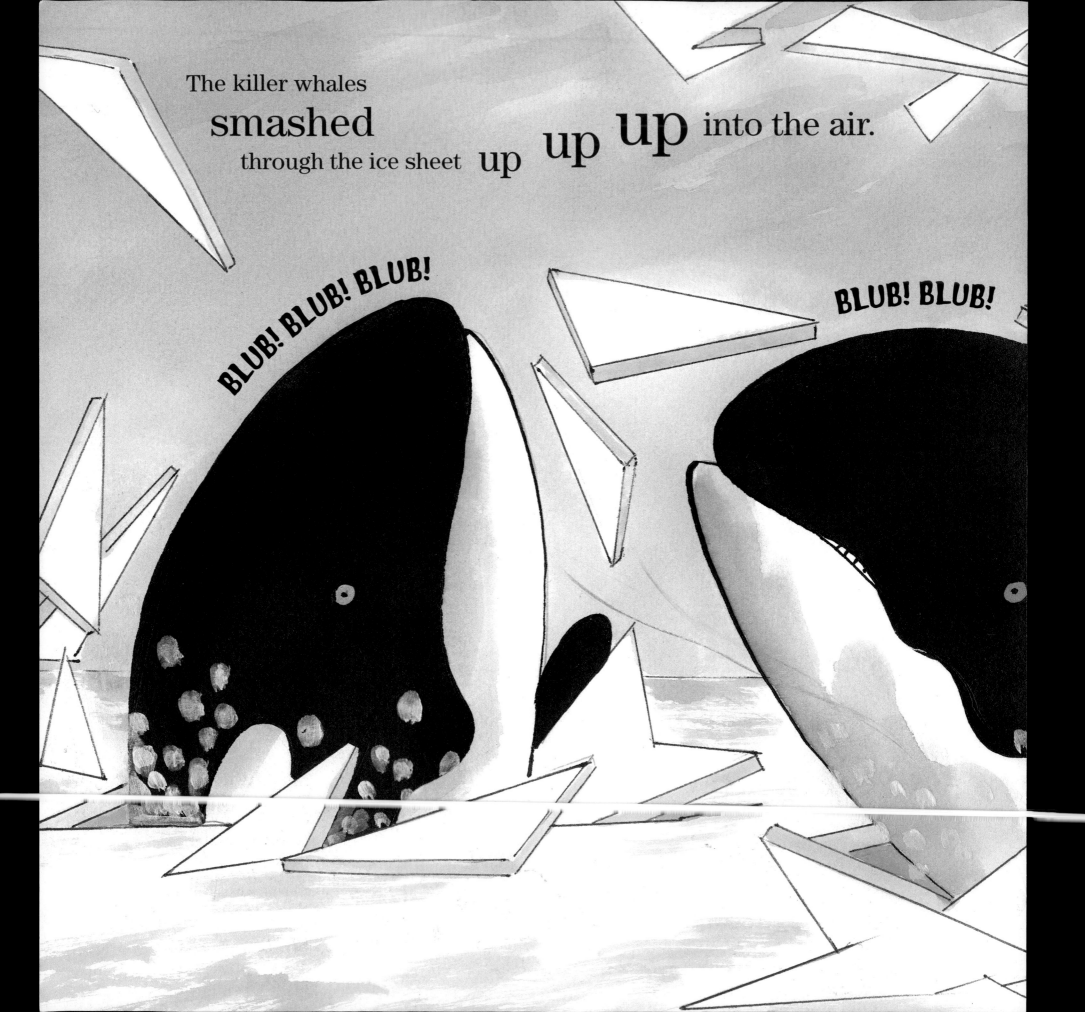

The first belly-flopped on to the ice. Then the more blubbery of the two landed on top of his poor friend.

As the sun was setting over the Arctic the cheeky little cub spotted a **very odd**-looking animal he had never seen before.

The poor man leaped backwards and fell with a giant plop into the sea.

"Noooooooooo!"

The water was SO cold that when he clambered out he was encased in a block of ice.

The man was furious. His face glowed bright red like a tomato, and the ice soon began to melt. *"In all my years I have never met such a badly-behaved animal! I've had...*

*an octopus **tickle** me,*

*been **sat on** by a rhinoceros and*

*once a family of gorillas **ate** my **underpants!!!***

*But **YOU** are the **worst!"***

As the little cub watched the helicopter leave, all the animals gathered.

Now they were going to **miss** their moment of **FAME**.

That night the little cub trudged slowly back home.

But as he entered his snow cave…

The little cub's fur stood up on end as if he'd been hit by a **bolt of lightning.**

"Aargh!"

Mama Bear was right.
He didn't like it
one bit.

The little cub had learned a **big lesson**.
From that moment he promised **never**,
ever, to go boo again.

Well maybe one
last time…

"BOO!"

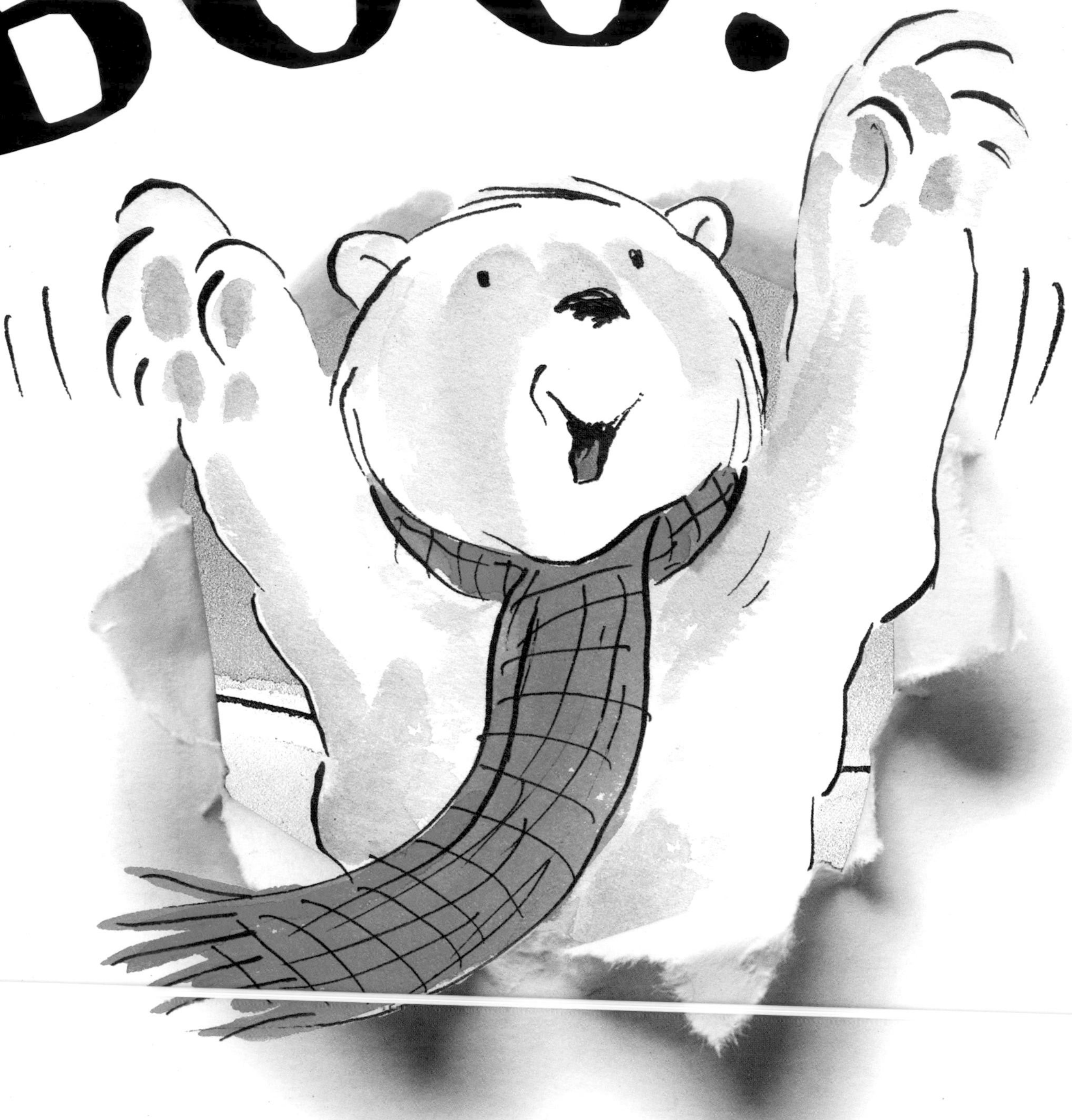